D0928452

LILLIBET
The Monster Vet

For Simon and the vets at Cannon Hill, Southgate
J.W.

For the de Leeu-Schroeder Family, Klub Barbounia members
K.P.

ORCHARD BOOKS
338 Euston Road, London NW1 3BH
Orchard Books Australia
Level 17/207 Kent Street, Sydney, NSW 2000
ISBN 1 84362 145 2 (paperback)
First published in Great Britain in 2004
First paperback publication in 2005
Text © Jeanne Willis 2004
Illustrations © Korky Paul 2004
The rights of Jeanne Willis to be identified as the author
and of Korky Paul to be identified as the illustrator of this
work have been asserted by them in accordance with the
Copyright, Designs and Patents Act, 1988.
A CIP catalogue record for this book is available from
the British Library.
1 3 5 7 9 10 8 6 4 2 (paperback)
Printed and bound in China
Orchard Books is a division of Hachette Children's Books

LILLIBET

The Monster Vet

Jeanne Willis * Korky Paul

ORCHARD BOOKS

LILLIBET

The Monster Vet

Let me through! I'm Lillibet,
The world's most famous Monster Vet.
I cure the beasts no one will touch —
Three-headed dogs, werewolves and such.

People say, "You must be brave
To treat a monster in its cave.
You might be gobbled up alive!"
I always tell them, "I'll survive."

I speak their language, that's the trick.

If some poor monster feels sick

I'll say to him, "What's wrong, my friend?

Just point to where it hurts, which end?"

Some patients are extremely shy.
I think that they would rather die
Than show their faces. I confess
It tried my patience in Loch Ness.

The monster wouldn't leave the lake,
Not even for some Dundee cake.
It was afraid that folk would stare,
Or film it in its underwear.

Night visits were the only way
(Too many tourists in the day).
By torchlight then, I had to come
And dress the boil on Nessy's bum.

The Yeti's really very sweet.
He had such trouble with his feet.
They're very big and yet his shoes
Were very small. He wore size two's.

I trimmed his bunion and his corn
And, noticing his shoes were worn,
I prescribed a *bigger* pair
That let out sweat and let in air.

The Phoenix bird just never learns,
I'm often treating her for burns.
She's always playing fireside games.
I warned her, "You'll go up in flames!"

The giant squid? He drove me mad
With all the stomach-aches he had.
I said, "Drink rum in *little* sips,
You're eating far too many ships."

I told him, "Watch the food you eat.
Have one yacht, not the whole darn fleet!
Eat sailors - they make healthy snacks -
Though fat ones may cause heart attacks."

I have to say my proudest feat
Was when I went to Ancient Crete.
In all the years I'd been a vet
It was my greatest challenge yet.

The phone went in my surgery.
King Minos said, "Hello, it's me.
My favourite bull has caught a chill.
He has a cough, he's very ill."

"A cattle vet is what you need,"
I told him, but he disagreed.
"He is a *monster* bull," he said,
"He's got a really massive head."

Reluctantly, I said I'd go,
I'd have to charge him double though,
To treat this poor, mis-shapen freak.
"No problem, love," he said in Greek.

I grabbed my passport. Off I flew,
Not knowing what I'd have to do.
The king was glad to see me there,
And showed me to the patient's lair.

"He's in that labyrinth," he said.
"Please hurry up - he's almost dead!"
He pushed me in and slammed the door.
"Prepare to meet the Minotaur!

"He'll eat you whole!" I heard him shout.
"It's like a maze, you can't get out.
 He just ate seven girls and boys."
(I thought I'd heard a screaming noise.)

I carried on. I wasn't scared,
I'm highly trained – I came prepared.
I marked the route with bandage roll
To guide me through the winding hole.

I marched off to the inner core
And heard a most tremendous roar.
And there he stood, half-man, half-beast,
I wasn't frightened in the least.

I asked him to lift up his vest
And then I listened to his chest.
He giggled, bless him. Good as gold.
He said, "That stethoscope is cold!"

His lungs and heart seemed very strong.
I asked him, "What is really wrong?"
"My cough is driving me insane!"
He said, "My throat's in dreadful pain."

I said, "Let's have a look. Say 'Ahh!'
Stick your tongue out nice and far.
That's very good, stay open wide."
I took my torch and peered inside.

I saw the problem straight away.
I treated it without delay.
His windpipe was severely blocked
With several objects. I was shocked.

34

I found a bike, a pram, a shoe
And several little children, too,
Still very much alive and well
As far as anyone could tell.

"I hate those kids!" the monster cried.
"They make me feel all sick inside.
I have no teeth. I cannot chew.
The worst thing is, I'm vegan, too."

"You need to convalesce," I said,
"In hospital - I'll book a bed.
And after, it would do no harm
To live your life out on a farm."

I called an ambulance. The king
Was not best pleased, the sulky thing.
The foolish man, for all his wealth,
Had sacrificed the creature's health.

"If you don't set this monster free
I'll have you done for cruelty,"
I said. "He needs fresh air and rest
And lots of grass. It's for the best."

King Minos cursed me, it is true.
He yelled, "I'll set the sphinx on you.
May Cyclops turn you into stone
And Hydra bite you to the bone!"

But when I met the monstrous three
They wanted to come home with me.
So off we went, my band of four,
Sphinx, Cyclops, Hydra, Minotaur.

They lived with me in Palmer's Mews.
I fed them on Greek barbecues.
They soon got well, but even so
Those monsters didn't want to go.

I trained them up to work for me —
They studied Beast Biology.
Now three are vets and one's a nurse.
You need an op? You could do worse!

Written by Jeanne Willis * Illustrated by Korky Paul

All priced at £3.99 each

Crazy Jobs are available from all good book shops, or can be ordered direct
from the publisher: Orchard Books, PO BOX 29, Douglas IM99 1BQ
Credit card orders please telephone 01624 836000
or fax 01624 837033 or visit our Internet site: www.wattspub.co.uk
or e-mail: bookshop@enterprise.net for details.

To order please quote title, author and ISBN
and your full name and address.
Cheques and postal orders should be made payable to 'Bookpost plc.'
Postage and packing is FREE within the UK
(overseas customers should add £1.00 per book).
Prices and availability are subject to change.